Adele Parks worked in [...] her first novel in 2000. Since then, her many *Sunday Times* bestsellers, including the No. 1 bestsellers, *Lies Lies Lies* and *Just My Luck*, have been translated into twenty-six different languages, and have sold 3.5 million copies. Adele spent her adult life in Italy, Botswana and London until 2005 when she moved to Guildford, where she now lives with her husband and son.

For more information visit **www.adeleparks.com** where you can sign up to receive Adele's newsletter. You can also find her on Facebook **www.facebook.com/OfficialAdeleParks** and follow her on Twitter **@adeleparks**.

Adele PARKS

HAPPY FAMILIES

REVIEW

Copyright © 2008 Adele Parks

The right of Adele Parks to be identified as the Author of
the Work has been asserted by her in accordance with the
Copyright, Designs and Patents Act 1988.

First published in Great Britain in 2008
by PENGUIN BOOKS

This edition published in Great Britain in 2012
by HEADLINE REVIEW
An imprint of HEADLINE PUBLISHING GROUP

8

Cataloguing in Publication Data is available from the British Library

ISBN 978 0 7553 9440 1

Typeset in Garamond MT

Printed and bound in Great Britain by Clays Ltd, Elcograf S.p.A.

MIX
Paper from
responsible sources
FSC® C104740

Headline's policy is to use papers that are natural, renewable and recyclable
products and made from wood grown in well-managed forests and other
controlled sources. The logging and manufacturing processes are expected
to conform to the environmental regulations of the country of origin.

HEADLINE PUBLISHING GROUP
An Hachette UK Company
Carmelite House
50 Victoria Embankment
London EC4Y 0DZ

www.headline.co.uk
www.hachette.co.uk

1

3 September

Lisa liked to be in control. She could control most things. Like her ironing basket – she found it easy to stay on top of that, and most other women found it hard, which just goes to show what a great control freak she was. She controlled her soap-watching. Well, really, she just gave in to that. She never missed an episode of *EastEnders* or *Coronation Street*. And she had a good idea about the main plots in *Emmerdale* and *Holby City* too. She could control what went into her kid's lunchboxes – not too much junk, brown bread sandwiches, yogurt and carrot sticks – although she could not control what they really ate. For all she knew, they chucked away the fruit and spent their pocket money on crisps.

Controlling her family was the hard bit. The important bit and the hard bit. She liked to think she was in control of Kerry (aged fifteen), Paula (aged twelve) and Jack (aged eleven).

They were good kids, largely, but you could never be sure.

Lisa lived in fear of a teenage pregnancy, a drug or drink problem or a not very happy copper standing at the door.

She hadn't always been like this. Lisa used to be very positive, about her now and her future. But two years ago, just before her fortieth birthday, her husband of fifteen years had said goodbye.

Something like that shakes you up. It takes your trust away, your trust in the world. It seemed a serious thing to do just to get out of buying a birthday present. She'd have been happy enough with bubble bath or a box of chocolates.

While Lisa had been divorced for two years now, it still surprised her. She'd thought she would always be married to Keith. How was it possible that after fifteen years of being married you could stop being married suddenly? That was a silly question. Of course Lisa knew how it was possible. Your husband runs off with a woman with big breasts. Too big. Silly big. Papers are signed. You're divorced. It's as simple as that. But it's not simple at all, not really – not in Lisa's heart.

Lisa didn't fall apart. She didn't have time,

with three kids to care for. Falling apart over a broken relationship is something you can only do when you are still a kid yourself. Or if you are a star, and *Heat* magazine will put your photo on their cover. If not, you just have to get on with it.

Her family was there for her. At least, they all acted just as she expected. That was a comfort of sorts, after Keith had acted so oddly.

Her mother and father went into shock. They'd been married for forty-five years. There had never been a divorce in the family. Well, except for Granny Hills and Uncle Terry and cousin Clare (she'd been divorced twice). They meant there had never been a divorce in the close family. They didn't mean her to but Lisa got the feeling she'd let them down. It was a bit like receiving her O level results when she was sixteen. Everyone said she'd tried her best. No one looked that pleased with the results.

Her father's hair turned white almost overnight. Her mother said it was the shock. Lisa believed it was because he'd stopped using that stupid dye her mum bought from Boots.

Her sister, Carol, was the posh one in the family. She'd married a teacher. He was now a headmaster, and somehow this had changed things. Carol had lunch and dinner now. The rest of the family were still happy with dinner and tea, with sometimes the odd bit of supper too. Carol no longer liked a bargain, she liked value for money. Carol used napkins at every meal. The rest of the family used kitchen roll, but only on special occasions.

Carol had not been happy when Keith left Lisa. She took it as a personal slight. In fact, as she took it so badly, Lisa felt she had to play down the whole thing. Lisa had to pretend it didn't matter much. She pretended that selling her house, going out to work and being alone was all OK. She didn't want to upset Carol any more. She was sick of Carol ranting.

But it did matter.

John, Lisa's little brother, had the best reaction. He didn't seem to have noticed Lisa was divorced at all. The divorce didn't have anything to do with booze or women, which were his hobbies. John was thirty-eight and only ever thought about himself. He was still single and dead happy to be so. His longest ever relationship had lasted two months and he was proud of that. Lisa would be dying of shame. She told him this.

'That's the difference between men and women,' he said. 'If I play around, I'm a stud. If you do, you are a slapper.'

4

Lisa told her brother he was a sexist pig. He grinned, thinking she was being nice.

'That's not fair,' said Lisa. But then she remembered it's also not fair that Angelina Jolie gets to have babies with Brad Pitt. Life is many things. It can be funny, interesting, hard and sad, but it's never fair.

Then there were the children. They *seemed* OK. But everyone said Lisa *seemed* OK. Was OK good enough? They seemed to understand it when their dad said he needed to be with the Big Breasted Woman from the accounts team at his work. More than he needed to be with them or his wife of fifteen years. He actually said he needed to be with Helen, but Lisa couldn't bring herself to use the woman's name. It made her seem . . . well, human. Lisa called her the Big Breasted Woman Who Replaced Me, or just the Big Breasted Woman for short.

The kids hadn't turned to crime, and that was odd, because all the newspapers said kids from broken homes were trouble. Lisa's kids were fine, which goes to show you can't believe everything you read. The promise of two sets of birthday and Christmas presents really helped.

Lisa had had a very controlled morning. She had sorted the wash into light clothes and dark.

She'd put on the darks. There were always more darks, the kids all lived in jeans. She'd cleaned the kitchen, made beds, run round with the hoover and the duster. She'd even washed the floor in the porch. She had everything under control. So why had it seemed such a terrible morning?

Lisa knew why. There'd been no noise. She was used to noise. She didn't like noise but she expected it, lots of it. Today the only noise had been her voice.

'Now then, Lisa, I think it's time to clean out your sock drawer,' she'd said. And then she'd said back to herself, 'Good idea.'

But it was not a good idea. Manic cleaning and talking to yourself are signs of madness. Think of the Big Brother House. When a contestant starts to overdo the polishing, scrubbing, tidying, you know they are losing it, and it's the same thing with talking to yourself.

It was the first day of the new school term. The kids were all back at school and Lisa felt very alone. It was odd that she missed them. Lisa had spent the last six weeks begging for hush. But now that the new school term had started Lisa was not so sure. The silence of an empty house was about as welcome as heavy rain on sports day.

Lisa grumbled that the kids were always demanding things from her.

'Mum, I'm hungry. When's tea?'

'Mum, will you iron my top?'

'Mum, can you drive me to my friend's house?'

But in truth Lisa liked being needed. She had always been needed. Keith, her husband, had needed her first. But then he stopped needing her and became her ex-husband. Lisa felt the kids didn't need her like they used to. She knew the kids couldn't divorce her, as such. But they could leave. They *should* leave – that was natural. But what then, for Lisa? She had a new man in her life, Mark, but he was the independent sort. He didn't need her. She wasn't sure how long he'd want her for. Nothing was certain.

This year was the last school year for Kerry, unless Lisa could talk her into doing A levels. She might leave home in the next year or two. Lisa hated the idea. Paula was almost thirteen (going on thirty). Paula was more worldly than her mum. Lisa couldn't remember the last time Paula had needed her for anything other than money! And now Jack was at secondary school too.

This morning Lisa had wanted to walk him to

7

school. Jack went mad. He said his friends would laugh. The school was only up the road – not even as far as the chip shop. Lisa often sent him to buy chips. He was not a baby. He didn't need Lisa. But Lisa needed him. Lisa needed to be needed.

She felt useless.

2

3 September

Lisa called Carol, her big sister. Lisa always called Carol if she was feeling a bit down. Lisa thought Carol would cheer her up, but that was a mistake. Carol never made Lisa feel better, but Lisa never learned! The good news was that sometimes Carol could boss Lisa out of a bad mood.

'It's a good thing that the kids can be on their own more,' said Carol. Carol sounded so sure of herself. Lisa was never sure of herself.

'Is it?' asks Lisa.

'Yes. You'll have more time to yourself.'

'But I don't want more time to myself,' said Lisa. 'I have too much time to myself as it is.' Lisa liked using her time to look after her family.

'You can do more hours at work. The extra cash will come in handy,' said Carol.

This was true but not a comfort. No one liked to be reminded that they needed more cash, and no one liked to think that they had to work harder. Lisa worked hard enough as it was. She was a single mum. Carol didn't understand how much work that was. Carol was a rare thing. Carol was happily married.

But Lisa did enjoy her job. She worked in a small café just up the road. It was not a posh café, more of a grotty caff. It was not the sort of place that sold millions of different types of coffee. The coffee came out of a jar and you just had to add boiling water. There were no posh sandwiches with tiny tomatoes and smelly cheeses. It was the sort of place that sold everything fried and with chips: fried egg and chips, fried bacon and chips, fried Mars bar and chips. The place was even called 'N Chips'.

Lisa had worked at 'N Chips' since her divorce. Before that she'd been a stay-at-home mum. Keith did not like her going out to work. He said he was the money-maker, but that changed when he left with the Big Breasted Woman. Then he wanted Lisa to make her own money.

It was not a bad little job. The boss, Dave, was good about Lisa changing hours if she ever needed to pop into the school or take one of the kids to the dentist. Dave understood about bringing up kids alone. His mother had done it and his sister was doing it. Who'd have thought Lisa would ever be so fashionable?

Dave and his wife didn't have kids. They were getting on a bit now. They were Lisa's age and too old to bother. Lisa had never asked Dave if they'd ever wanted kids. It was not the sort of thing *she* would ask. Paula would, given the chance. Paula was at an age where nothing was private.

For example, the other day Paula had asked Lisa if Lisa had 'sexual relations' with her boyfriend, Mark. Lisa was very embarrassed, even though Mark had been part of their lives for a few months now. Wasn't that the wrong way round? Paula had had 'the talk' at school. She'd had a good idea about the birds and the bees before she'd had the proper lesson at school. But now she'd had the lesson she felt totally grown-up. Paula saw a chance to embarrass and confuse her mum. Every kid loves to do that! After asking about her mum's personal life she quickly asked, 'Can I have my belly-button pierced?'

Lisa was so hot and bothered by the 'sexual relations' question that she said she'd think about the piercing. For ages she'd said, 'No. No. No,' but anything to change the subject.

Later, when Lisa had time to think about it, she realized she'd been tricked.

For the record, Mark and Lisa were having sex. Thank you for your interest! Lisa was forty-two, with three kids and a divorce under her belt. She was officially not-so-young, not-so-free and not-so-single. She was also not-so-comfortable talking about her sex life with her young daughter – or her mother, come to that. She wasn't modern enough to deal with it.

Lisa was never very modern. Even when she was young, she was old-fashioned. She was a nice girl who just wanted to settle down and have a family. She didn't regret it. She loved her family more than anything in the world.

She'd never thought about A levels like Kerry might. She'd never wanted her tummy-button pierced like Paula did. She'd never had an ambition to play football for Manchester United like Jack did. Maybe that's not surprising!

Her ambition had been to marry, then to live Happily Ever After, the way they do in fairy tales. Her problem was what was after 'After'.

Lisa thought that by the time she reached the age of forty-two, her only problem would be whether to use sew-on or iron-on labels to name her kids' school uniforms. Instead, she had to struggle with what she should call the man in her life.

'Husband' was so simple. But Mark was not her husband. Mark was a man who had come round to give her an estimate for converting the loft. And slowly but surely turned into ... Well. What?

The term boyfriend seemed so *young*. Lisa thought she was too old for a boyfriend. Her daughters talked about boyfriends. She wished they didn't! She wasn't ready for them to grow up!

Lisa's mother called Mark a toy-boy. Every time she said it, she nudged Lisa and winked. At moments like those Lisa had sympathy for her kids. Parents never stop showing you up! True, technically, Mark was a toy-boy, as he was five years younger than Lisa. But didn't toy-boys date older women for their money? Mark couldn't be in it for the money. Lisa had none. Her idea of a good investment was buying two lottery tickets.

Carol thought Lisa should call Mark her partner.

'As often as possible,' she said, 'to make it clear to everyone that he's yours. It's a competitive world and he's a catch.'

It sounded a bit desperate to Lisa. But even

the kids agreed with Carol. Single, Lisa was a drag. They didn't want to have to look after her in her old age. Jack had said so. The boy wasn't known for his tact! But 'partner' put Lisa in mind of cowboys – 'Howdy partner' – or people who liked people in their own hockey team.

Lisa's brother, John, said Lisa should call Mark her 'dude'. This was proof that he lived on a different planet from anyone else Lisa knew.

Lisa wondered how come *everyone* else seemed to know how to label her relationship. Where did her voice go?

Only Mark didn't seem to care what Lisa called him, as long as she did keep calling him, which was sweet. Men *are* sweet at the beginning, aren't they, thought Lisa. But, like cream cakes in a shop window, they go off.

3

10 September

Keith, Lisa's ex, visited her when the kids were at school, which was a surprise.

'What do you want?' she asked. He always wanted something.

He asked for a cup of tea, but she knew that there was something bigger. Lisa gave him a chipped mug. It wasn't as big a crime as him running off with the Big Breasted Woman, but it was something. She hoped he noticed. He dipped his biscuit and drank his tea. Then he gave her a booklet.

Right away Lisa was worried. The last papers he'd given her were divorce papers.

'What is it?' Lisa asked, sulkily.

'Some information about local night classes. There are lots to choose from: computer studies, sewing, cake-decorating, foreign languages. I thought you might be interested. You could do with a new challenge,' said Keith.

15

'Don't you think bringing up three kids on my own is challenge enough?' Lisa asked, crossly.

'Helen learnt all she knows from a night class on textiles,' said Keith.

Lisa knew the Big Breasted Woman studied textiles at some poxy night class. Keith had told her a million times. Lisa wanted to make a joke that Helen did have talents involving textiles such as cotton sheets. And that Helen probably did learn these talents in the night. His affair proved that. But Lisa resisted. She'd sound mean. Keith brought the worst out in Lisa – she was often angry around him.

Lots of things about Keith annoyed Lisa. One was that in the years they were married, he plodded along in his job at Carpet Land. He made an OK amount of money working on the sales team on the shop floor. Lisa and Keith had a pretty, but small, house. They went on a week's holiday every year to Spain or Greece. Their kids wore the 'must have' trainers that they wanted. Lisa and Keith managed. They had a nice enough, normal enough life.

Two months after leaving Lisa, Keith packed in his job at Carpet Land. He set up an interior design company, if you please! Of course it was the Big Breasted Woman's idea. She said there were lots of people who would pay loads of money just to be told where to scatter their cushions. Lisa was amazed by his cheek. Yes, the man knew about carpets, but that was *it*. He had never so much as held a paintbrush. Or a loo brush. Or a dustpan and brush, come to that.

But suddenly Keith was telling people about candles and colours. He told them how important it was to have a warm and welcoming hallway. He told them to buy fresh cut flowers. Lisa only had plastic ones. Keith had bought them for her about ten years ago. He'd said plastic were better, because you only had to buy one bunch in a lifetime. He'd changed his mind about that and many other things.

Last year Keith and the Big Breasted Woman had bought a five-bedroom house. They went on *three* holidays! Lisa and the kids had a week in Dorset. It rained every day.

Thinking of Keith's happiness made Lisa cross and bothered. How dare he come into her house and tell her she needed a challenge? Keith reached for the last biscuit on the plate and bit it. Lisa grabbed the biscuit out of his hand.

'I think you should go now,' she said.

Keith stood up. At the door he turned to Lisa

and said, 'Your curtains are old-fashioned. You should get some new ones.'

Lisa only just resisted beating him to death with the TV remote control.

When the kids got home from school, they saw the booklet about night classes that Keith had left behind. They said their father's idea was a good one. Lisa felt hurt that they agreed with him, but she couldn't say so. She would look childish if she did.

'It's good to exercise your brain. You owe it to yourself,' said Jack.

'You should do a course in accounts, Mum. Accountants are always minted. Every girl needs to have her own money. You can't rely on anyone, least of all men, to pay the bills,' added Kerry.

Lisa remembered saying these exact words herself. So it was hard to argue. Lisa spent a lot of time telling the kids that education was very important. She said education would help them find a happy future. She really believed that.

She didn't always believe the things she said to the kids.

She told them things that she *wanted* them to believe. She wanted them to believe in Father Christmas and the Tooth Fairy. It was a good way of getting them to behave. Lisa also told her girls that boys would like them *more* if they *didn't* wear padded bras and lip-gloss. Again, she thought it would be a good way of getting them to behave! Sadly, they didn't believe it either.

But they must have believed what Lisa said about education, because they said it back to her now.

'But I like my job. I don't want to retrain,' said Lisa.

'What do you like about it?' asked Paula.

'I enjoy chatting to the customers. I know that the overalls I wear to work aren't high fashion, but they hide my bumps and lumps and don't need ironing. That's important, because you cannot think how many times I smear or slop in a working day,' said Lisa.

The children stared at their mum. Lisa wondered if she had a large L for loser just above her head. Her children looked at her as though she had.

Lisa called Carol. Carol said. 'Well, I agree with Keith and the children. You could do more with your life.'

'But I've never wanted a high-flying job,' said Lisa. 'I'm happy at the café.'

'So you say.' Carol didn't sound as though she believed her.

'Why the sudden interest in my job?' asked Lisa.

'The kids are probably embarrassed by what you do now,' said Carol. Lisa thought that maybe *Carol* was embarrassed by her job.

Carol talked to their mum. Then their mum telephoned and said Lisa should do a course on flower-arranging. Cross again, Lisa pointed out that no one ever bought her flowers. No one ever had!

The doorbell rang.

'That will be Mark, I have to go,' said Lisa. She was glad of the excuse to get off the phone.

'Doesn't he have a key?' asked her mum.

'No.'

'Why not?'

'I've never given him one,' said Lisa.

'Why not?' asked her mum again.

Lisa hung up.

Mark and Lisa were not 'seeing' each other that night. It was not a date. Mark had popped by to look at the leaky tap in the bathroom. It only took him a minute to fix the drip. Lisa told him about her day and everyone wanting her to do a night class.

'Maybe I should do a course in DIY. Then I wouldn't have to call you for help every ten minutes,' joked Lisa.

'Good idea,' said Mark.

Lisa froze. Was Mark fed up with fixing things in her house? And did that mean he was fed up with her? She signed up for a DIY course, just in case Mark was planning his exit.

4

Lisa was worried about starting the DIY course. The only tool she knew how to use was a corkscrew. She was also worried she wouldn't even be able to find the college. Lisa didn't like to drive or catch a bus to anywhere new. She didn't like change or new things very much at all.

Carol said she must 'face her fears'. Lisa's biggest fear was arguing with her big sister. But she couldn't say this, as it would have led to a row. Clearly, facing her fears wasn't Lisa's thing.

Mark said he'd drive Lisa to the college. Maybe he was being kind. Or maybe he was just very keen for Lisa to do the DIY course. Was he was sick of her depending on him? Lisa thought she'd been very wise not to get too involved with Mark. OK, so she liked him a lot. But no one would ever guess, she'd never told him or anyone else. What was the point?

Keith had proved there was no point. It was best to keep things casual, like John did with his women.

'Thanks, dude,' said Lisa.

Mark gave her an odd look. There, now he'd know she wasn't serious about him! If she'd been serious about him, she would have said, 'Thanks, *partner*.'

Lisa made tea for the kids. Kerry was out somewhere. She had a new boyfriend. Lisa wanted to meet him. But Kerry said that was 'too heavy'. So Lisa hadn't met him yet. Lisa called Kerry on her mobile and made her promise she'd be home by nine.

Lisa had asked her brother John to sit with Paula and Jack. Paula was cross and hurt. She pointed out that she'd be thirteen in ten days and was more grown-up than her uncle. As she said this, John was rolling on the floor, fighting with Jack for the TV remote. They couldn't agree on which violent cartoon to watch.

'You're right. Make sure your Uncle John cleans his teeth before he goes to bed,' said Lisa.

On the way to the night class Lisa snapped at Mark. She was sure he was going the wrong way.

'We'll hit the teatime traffic. We'll be late,' she said. Then she added, 'Dude.' She wasn't sure she'd managed to sound casual. Stressing about traffic wasn't casual.

Mark stayed calm. 'Put the map away. I know where we're going. We have plenty of time,' he said.

Lisa tutted – she didn't believe him.

They got to college in ten minutes. They were early. Mark did not say, 'I told you so,' which was wise because Lisa was too nervous to be proved wrong.

He bought her a cup of coffee from a machine. It didn't taste very nice but Lisa didn't dare moan. He stayed with her until it was time for the class, and then walked her right to the door. He really was keen for her to take this class! He smiled and waved as though everything was fine. Lisa couldn't agree. She was so nervous that it was hard to put one foot in front of another. She completely forgot to call, 'Bye, dude.' She was a DIY virgin about to be sacrificed.

The tutor arrived and said everyone had to say who they were and why they were there. Someone made a joke about signing up for a DIY course, not philosophy. The tutor glared at the joker. He didn't like chat in his classroom. Lisa was happy with that. She didn't plan to make friends. Chatting with anyone would show her up as a complete nuts-and-bolts beginner. The shame! And she was a divorcee. Double shame! People would think that she was there because she didn't have a man in her life to hang pictures, which was not true. She had Mark. But for how long? Not for ever because there's no such thing.

Sometimes Lisa wondered why Mark was with her at all. She knew that the media were always saying women in their forties were still sexy. But Lisa was no Liz Hurley. Lisa was not much like Nigella Lawson or Carol Vorderman either. Lisa thought about celebs she might be like. She decided she was like Lassie. A bit of an old dog, in need of a haircut. But her bark was worse than her bite.

Lisa tried to put Mark out of her mind. Thinking about him made her nervous. Her tummy flipped. Was it happiness or fear?

Lisa looked around the room. She was pleased to see that the class was full of women. Some were pretty young things who wanted to be independent. Others were not so young. They were less likely to have a choice.

Lisa learnt the difference between screws and nails. It was something. It wasn't as hard as she had feared it might be. You just had to follow instructions. It was like reading a recipe.

At the coffee break a smiley woman told Lisa that custard creams were her favourite biscuits. Lisa didn't think this could be true when you could buy Hobnobs. The lady was just trying to chat. Lisa gave the lady her custard cream and asked her if she had any kids. The lady looked just like Lisa (size fourteen, big hips, no boobs), but she had earrings, lip-gloss and a good hair-cut. Therefore was like Lisa but sort of sexier, sort of better. Lisa wondered if she should visit a hairdresser. For the past ten years Lisa's mum had snipped away at her split ends.

The sort of sexier, sort of better woman was called Gill. She turned out to be a cheery divorcee.

'I'm well shot of my ex,' said Gill with a big grin. 'You'll understand that, Lisa.'

Lisa hadn't thought that being without Keith was a perk, but faced with the direct question, she couldn't deny it. Gill gave Lisa the number of her hairdresser. Then she made a cheeky comment about the 'total hunk' who was hang-ing around outside. She meant Mark!

Lisa didn't think of Mark as a total hunk. But looking at him now, it was as if it was the first time she'd seen him. She noticed that Mark was a fit thirty-seven-year-old. He had strong arms because his work was manual. He always had a tan because he liked to be outdoors. Somehow he found sun in England. The mix of the tan and the muscles made him stand out from other men. Most people Lisa knew were pale and run down. But Mark was also losing his hair a bit at the front and he had a very small rounding of the tummy. Lisa was glad. A full mop of hair like Tom Cruise, or a six-pack like James Bond, would have scared her.

Lisa went outside the classroom to talk to Mark. 'What are you still doing here?' she asked.

'I thought I'd stay close by. Just in case you didn't like the class and wanted to go home early,' said Mark.

'I'm not giving up that soon!' said Lisa.

'I hoped not, but I was, you know, a bit worried about you.' Mark looked a bit red in the face, not very casual at all. 'Anyway, Kerry's just called. She wants a lift. I'm going to pick her up now if you are OK. I'll be back here for you later.'

Gill winked at Lisa and said, 'Lucky cow.'

It was nice for Lisa to think sexy Gill was a bit jealous of Lisa's boyfriend, partner, dude – whatever Mark was.

After the class Lisa found Kerry waiting with Mark. She was surprised. She'd thought Kerry would want to go straight home, not wait around for Lisa. It was clear that Kerry had something on her mind. It wasn't often that she chose to hunt out her mum to spend time with her. After all, they invented TV years ago.

'Do you need your pocket money early?' asked Lisa.

'No.' Kerry sounded hurt at the suggestion that her reasons for coming to see her mum were selfish.

Mark said he'd bring the car round to the front and meet them there. He was giving them space.

'How was your date?' asked Lisa.

'It wasn't a date,' said Kerry. She turned pink. 'People don't date in this millennium. We hang out together.'

Lisa knew for a fact that people did still go on dates. She'd read it in her magazines. People like her and Mark might not date, though. They'd had to do their dating over fish-finger teas and kids' homework. But other people definitely dated. Lisa didn't say so, though.

'So how was the hanging out?' she asked.

'OK,' muttered Kerry.

Lisa would have left the conversation there. She didn't often expect much more than the odd word when she was talking with her kids.

But she happened to glance at Kerry. Kerry had two spots of red on her cheeks and she was blinking back tears.

'Did you have a row?' asked Lisa. She wanted to sound patient. A teenage row was nothing on the grand scale, but for Kerry it would be the end of the world.

'Yes. He's hanging out with Chloe Jackson now,' said Kerry.

'Oh, love, I'm sorry,' said Lisa. She tried to put her arm around Kerry but her hands were full with large textbooks and a drill.

'I'm not,' said Kerry. But Lisa wasn't fooled. They spotted Mark's car and got in without another word.

Oh drat, thought Lisa. There was one thing worse than not being needed: being needed and being no help.

5

Paula was officially a teenager. She had been acting like one for years. She had sulked, slammed doors and worn short skirts for a long time, but still, it was an important day.

Paula was happy with the earrings and new top Lisa had bought but said Keith had promised her an iPod. Lisa didn't know what an iPod was but she knew it cost a lot. Lisa was cross with him for being able to outdo her, but happy that Paula was going to do well out of it. Nothing was ever simple for her now. Kerry gave Paula a CD. It didn't come with a smile. She was still heartbroken about that boy hanging out with Chloe Jackson. Jack handed over a book token (that Lisa had bought).

Paula spent ages in the bathroom and came out wearing loads of make-up. She looked like someone off an MTV pop video. Lisa sighed and felt old. She didn't have the heart to row with Paula on her birthday, so she pretended not to see.

Lisa had invited all the family for tea. She didn't think they would all say yes, but sadly they did. John said he'd bring a date. That was thirteen to feed and seat. Oh dear! Matters were made worse when Paula asked if she could invite her dad. Lisa wanted to say no but spat out 'yes'. Then Keith invited the Big Breasted Woman and his parents. Lisa hated herself for saying, 'The more the merrier.' She meant to say, 'Get stuffed.'

Lisa had planned to pass around a plate of sausage rolls and some egg sandwiches. She changed her mind, now that the Big Breasted Woman was coming. She went to Marks & Spencer and bought their great party packs of food. She nipped to Argos and bought two new tea-sets because she didn't own enough matching plates. She panicked as she passed the newsagent, and bought a bumper pack of streamers and balloons. Paula's teenage tea party cost about the same as Lisa's wedding reception. At this rate Lisa thought she would have to sell a kidney to pay for Kerry's twenty-first.

Lisa called Gill from the DIY class. It was on

the offchance. They didn't know each other well yet, but Lisa thought they would be good friends, given time. And Lisa would need a friend at this tea party. Besides, her family were always better behaved in front of guests.

Lisa's mum and dad arrived first. John and his lady arrived next. Lisa didn't bother to learn her name. Like all the rest of John's girl-friends, she was nice, happy and hopeful. But it wouldn't last – a week or ten days at the most. John gave Paula a bottle of sparkly wine. Paula shouted, 'Wicked.' Lisa shouted, 'No way,' and quickly took it off her.

Carol and her family turned up with a big present. Then Gill arrived into the chaos. Keith and the add-ons arrived next. The Big Breasted Woman looked wonderful. She exercised a lot. Her credit card, that was! It was always being used. She had expensive hair, clothes and maybe even plastic surgery. Lisa wished she'd put on some lipstick. She was still red and sweaty from blowing up party balloons – not a great look.

Paula opened her gifts. Then the kids went up to their bedrooms to play noisily. The adults sat in the front room in silence. Everyone, other than Keith, seemed to know that this modern way to divorce (all one big happy family) was difficult to manage. The old way (never speaking again) would suit Lisa fine.

It did not feel like a party. More like a funeral. Keith's parents often slagged off the Big Breasted Woman to Lisa. They also slagged off Lisa to the Big Breasted Woman, so they were tense. Lisa's mother shot Keith's mother evil looks. She hadn't forgiven her for going to the Big Breasted Woman's wedding. Carol talked loudly about the dangers of cosmetic surgery. She stared meaningfully at the big breasts. Only Gill and John chatted happily, but even that upset John's date.

Lisa was worried about the bite-size flans that were part of the party pack from Marks & Spencer. They smelt a bit funny. Carol sniffed them and took a bite. She pronounced them delicious. It was impossible to argue. Lisa offered Keith a beer. The Big Breasted Woman said he never drank out of cans (a lie). Lisa offered her a wine.

'I don't drink sweet wines,' she said. Neither of them touched Lisa's spread. 'We're going on to a really good restaurant, later,' said the Big Breasted Woman.

Lisa wondered whether a judge would understand if she used a small strawberry flan to batter the Big Breasted Woman to death.

The hands on the clock seemed to be going backwards. The doorbell rang. Lisa was surprised to see Mark – she'd forgotten she'd invited him. She hadn't thought he'd come to a boring teenage party. Surely he had better things to do with his time? She'd only thrown the invite out at the last minute. But here he was.

Kerry, Paula and Jack ran down the stairs. They were so pleased to see him. Mark marched into the front room with a crate of expensive bottled beer and four bottles of champagne.

'I know Paula can't actually enjoy this but we'll toast her and she can keep the cork,' he said. He winked at Paula and passed her an envelope. 'This *is* for you to enjoy though.'

'Tickets to a Mika gig!' She squealed and hugged him. 'That is just the coolest. Thank you!'

Lisa stared at Mark, unable to hide from the fact that his arrival had got the party going. When she said so to Carol, Carol shrugged and said, 'It always does. Haven't you noticed?'

No, she hadn't noticed. She hadn't given it much thought.

Back in the living room, things were more relaxed. The kids had all come downstairs to stay, happy to be around Mark. Even the Big

Breasted Woman had a smile on her face. Was she trying to pretend to be a nice human being? Well, she could try all she liked. Mark knew better. Lisa had spent many months telling Mark what a horrible person the Big Breasted Woman was. He wasn't going to be fooled by a flash of white teeth and cleavage. He had more to him than that. Mark wasn't a white teeth and big boobs sort of man. He couldn't be, he was with Lisa. Her teeth were greyish. The result of a 1970s childhood and NHS dentists. And her cleavage was non-existent. Her nickname at school had been 'Ironing Board', she was that flat.

Lisa was handing out glasses of fizz and plates of pastry. The phone rang. She shouted for Paula to answer it.

'It will be for you, Paula. Someone wishing you happy birthday.'

'Like who? Everyone we know is here,' said Paula. She didn't want to have to move from in front of the TV.

Kerry suddenly appeared from nowhere. She snatched up the phone handset, went into the downstairs loo and closed the door with a firm bang.

'All back on with the boyfriend, I guess,' said Mark to Lisa.

'I suppose so. She hasn't mentioned any-thing.'

'Teenagers don't, do they?' added Carol. 'Now come on. Hurry up with that food. Dad thinks his throat has been cut, he's that hungry.'

6

10 October

The party went well. All the food was eaten and all the drink was drunk and no one hit anyone or even threw any outright insults. A great success as far as a family party went. But things had gone downhill since then.

Lisa had had a very bad couple of weeks. It seemed unlikely that Kerry had made it up with her boyfriend. After an hour and a half she had come out of the downstairs loo looking weepy. When Lisa asked her what was wrong she said, 'Nothing!' But in a way that meant *everything*. And Paula was a teenager now too, which is never good news for a parent. Jack had been picked for the school football team. This *was* good news, but Lisa had fallen asleep while watching the match on Saturday. He hadn't forgiven her for missing his goal. His cold angry silence was different from the girls' noisy rows, but still awful.

Lisa rang Carol and confessed to falling asleep on the sidelines.

'Are you ill?' asked Carol.

Carol was never ill. She said she hadn't got time to be ill. She also hadn't got time for people who were ill. She didn't say so – she didn't have to. Her actions spoke louder than words. When Carol's husband broke his arm last year, she said he'd done it on purpose to get out of painting the front room. Except that Carol called the front room a lounge now. If Bill had slipped on ice and fallen under a moving bike on purpose it didn't work. Carol made him paint with his left hand. Being ill was a weakness as far as Carol was concerned.

'I have been feeling a bit off,' said Lisa. 'I think I have a tummy bug. I've a temperature. It comes and goes.'

'Never heard of that,' said Carol. And because Carol hadn't heard of it she meant it didn't exist.

'I've been feeling really sick and I'm washed out. I haven't the energy to deal with moody kids.'

'It's the Change,' said Carol. She sounded pleased to have solved the mystery.

'I beg your pardon?' said Lisa. She was not pleased with this idea at all.

'You're menopausal. Hot flushes and tired-ness are signs. Plus you've been really moody recently. You say the kids are moody, but you're far worse,' said Carol.

Lisa was not sure if this was true. But she was not sure if it was untrue either. Last night, watching TV with Mark, she had cried at an advert that had kittens in it. They weren't being mistreated. They were being fed on the brand that eight out of ten cats prefer. She *was* being more than a little emotional. She was confused about so many things.

The children growing up and not needing her was a worry. What would she do with her life after they'd all left home? And what was the matter with Kerry? Shouldn't she be over her heartbreak by now? It had been days now, and she was a teenager – she should have moved on. Lisa couldn't think that the DIY course would lead her to a new career. Besides, she didn't want a new career. She liked her old one. She liked being a mum. She quickly added up how many years it would be before she was a granny. At least another ten. It was too long. Yet at the same time she wasn't anywhere near ready to be a granny!

Lisa was also still in pain over her split from Keith. It wasn't that she still missed *him*. He hadn't been that great for quite a few years of her marriage. She'd more or less been on her own for about five years before he left. It just left her feeling too ... What was the word? Open? Unprotected? Vulnerable?

The truth was Lisa was nervous that the party had only got going when Mark arrived. She was enjoying having him around far too much. It couldn't be a good thing, getting involved with a younger man. He wouldn't stay forever. She didn't know why he'd stayed this long. As usual when these thoughts flooded into Lisa's head, she ignored them.

'I'm too young for the menopause,' said Lisa, hotly.

'It happens to some people earlier than others,' said Carol. Was she enjoying this?

Lisa wanted to ask Carol if early menopause was a family trait. Had Carol been through it? But she was too embarrassed. Carol and Lisa had never, ever talked about anything like that. Between them they'd been through five pregnancies. In all that time they'd pretended to be like Barbie dolls (at least 'down there'). Sadly, neither of them had Barbie-like pert boobs or tiny waists.

As soon as Lisa put down the phone she went on the internet and did a search on 'menopause'. She didn't like what she found. Maybe she was closer to being a granny than she'd thought! She was getting old before her time. It wasn't fair!

Then Lisa called Gill. Lisa knew that Gill was the perfect person to call. Their friendship had really developed in just a few weeks. Lisa could pick up the phone and talk about hot flushes with Gill and be honest.

'What makes you think you're menopausal?' asked Gill.

'I went on the web. I looked up the symptoms. I have about thirty of the possible thirty-five!' Lisa wanted to cry. She didn't want to get old. Who does?

'Read the list to me,' said Gill.

'Hot flushes, trouble sleeping and night sweats,' said Lisa.

'That's probably just because the totally fab Mark stays over at your place more often than not. You've forgotten that it's sweaty sleeping with someone else in the bed,' said Gill.

'You paint such a romantic picture,' said Lisa. She read more from her list. 'Irregular heart-beat.'

'I'd put that down to Mark too. His smile makes *my* heart flutter,' said Gill.

'Mood swings, sudden tears,' said Lisa.

'Is that a warning?' asked Gill.

'Irritability,' Lisa said with some anger. Why couldn't Gill take this seriously?

Lisa skipped over the next two symptoms. One was loss of sex drive. She didn't have a problem there. The other had to do with what her mum called her 'front bottom'. She couldn't bring herself to say the words over the phone. Face to face and a glass of wine in hand maybe, but not now.

Lisa read on. 'Tiredness, anxiety, feelings of dread, difficulty in concentrating, memory lapses.'

'Lisa, maybe this isn't the menopause, maybe this is your personality,' said Gill.

She was trying to be helpful.

Gill was not going to be serious. She often laughed when Lisa had a moan. It was one of the things Lisa liked about her. Lisa decided to shut up. She didn't tell Gill about her sore boobs or mucked-up cycle. The mucked-up cycle had been going on for a couple of months now. Lisa hadn't wanted to face the fact. What was the point in talking about it? It was the menopause. Cold hard fact. Lisa would pop to Boots and see if there were any vitamins that would help.

'How are things with you?' Lisa asked to be polite.

'Your brother rang me and asked me for a date,' said Gill.

'What? I hope you told him where to get off! John's a cheating, many-timing rat. I wouldn't wish him on my worst enemy, let alone my new friend. He's selfish, lazy commitment-phobic and yet women just melt. I don't get it,' said Lisa.

'It's his smile,' said Gill. 'He has a lovely smile.'

'Really? I think he always looks smug. Still, well done you, for telling him to hop it,' said Lisa.

'I said yes, actually,' said Gill.

'Oh.'

Although Gill had married, divorced and had kids, she wasn't like Lisa. Gill hadn't been worn down with worry about school tests, hearing tests, swimming lessons and other mum stuff. She looked about ten years younger than Lisa and had a decent job as the manager at Next in the High Street.

The bad news was that she still secretly believed in 'the one'. Even though she'd rowed with her old 'one' about who got the furniture.

'I thought you were OK with this. He said

you gave him my number,' said Gill.

'Well, he lied. Get used to it.' First of many, no doubt. 'He must have nosed through my address book while he was babysitting when I was at my night class,' said Lisa.

'He's taking me to that new Italian in town,' said Gill. She sounded happy.

'Order something expensive,' said Lisa. She sounded cross.

Since Lisa was fourteen, John had dated a number of her friends. It always ended badly. Lisa's friends never wanted to admit they'd been taken for a fool or that John was a rat. So, oddly, Lisa always got the blame. She'd lost more friends through John's romantic adventures than she cared to remember.

'He breaks hearts,' said Lisa.

But she knew she was wasting her breath. No one ever learnt from anyone else's mistakes, and few of us learn from our own. Lisa was not looking forward to another friend getting hurt.

'I don't think you should go on the date,' said Lisa.

Gill was huffy. 'You need to learn to trust again. Your problem is you can no longer see chance or even goodness *anywhere*.'

'That's not true,' said Lisa, hurt.

'Yes, it is. Look at the way you treat Mark,' said Gill.

'I don't treat Mark badly.'

'You hardly know he's there, Lisa! You've just talked about your imaginary menopause for longer than you've ever talked to me about Mark.'

Really? That couldn't be right, could it?

'You should enjoy this new love,' said Gill.

What was she talking about? New love? What did Mark have to do with love? Mark was a fling, a stopgap, something other than Keith. That was all.

Gill had not finished. 'And one more thing. You'd better buy a pregnancy test. Just in case.'

With that she hung up the phone.

7

17 October

Lisa's boss and his wife had gone on holiday and left Lisa in charge of running the café. She couldn't believe that Dave trusted her so much. When he'd dropped off the keys at Lisa's house he had looked worried. Maybe he couldn't believe he trusted Lisa either.

Lisa would not be working alone. Betty (who had worked at 'N Chips' since forever) was coming in every day to help. She was very old, so she wouldn't be much help with serving or cleaning. But Betty was great at scaring people into buying things they didn't really want. She told them chips were good for them. She told them they needed fattening up. People loved it. It was a gift. With Betty around they'd do a good trade.

This wasn't a good time for extra duties at work. Lisa was in the middle of a serious 'can-we-get-a-puppy-for-Christmas?' debate with Jack.

'I know dogs are for life, not just for Christmas. That's what I like about them,' he said over and over again.

Then he'd look sadly at the picture of his dad that he kept on his bedside table.

Lisa thought he might be messing around with this emotional blackmail stuff, but she might not be strong enough to turn him down. What if he did need a dog to feel safe and she had ignored his plea? It might not be a scam. Maybe he'd like a Labrador. Lisa told herself she'd lose weight walking it. She didn't believe Jack would walk the dog – at least, not after the first week, whatever he promised. She wasn't born yesterday.

Also, Lisa was fighting early menopause. It was official. When she'd asked the teenager who was serving at Boots if there were vitamins to help with the menopause the teenager hadn't said, 'You're too young!' She'd just pointed to the shelf. There, Lisa had consulted a professional! Gill was out of her mind to talk about pregnancy tests. Lisa was menopausal, closer to being a granny than a mum.

Also she had a lot of homework from her DIY course. And her friend was dating her silly, careless brother, and then there was Mark.

Gill said Lisa took Mark for granted. Was that

true? It wasn't that Lisa was too confident. The opposite! Lisa didn't want to start to depend on Mark in case he went away. OK, at the moment he was always around. Right now, he was bringing Lisa chocolate. He checked that Jack was using the internet for homework, and just homework! He made Kerry and Paula laugh (often a superhuman thing). But for how long?

Lisa was worried that Mark's kindness would not last. She was keeping her distance. Just because he'd never done anything to hurt Lisa *yet* didn't mean he was not going to at some point. Did it? Look at Keith.

But Keith was not a good comparison. Hand on heart, he'd never have got the 'Husband of the Year' award. Before running off with the Big Breasted Woman he hadn't been too bad. He hadn't beaten her or taken drugs. But he hadn't been too good either. Keith had never been caring or kind like Mark was. Even before he had left with the Big Breasted Woman, Lisa had often been lonely.

Lisa thought about Mark all morning. She thought about him as she checked stock, cleaned ovens and fried chips. Paula came into the café at lunchtime with her spotty mates. Lisa made them all eat apples. She had brought the apples from home. Paula rolled her eyes. She said her mum was 'total sad'. Paula was shy about her mum openly caring. It was a teenage thing. But Lisa knew it was important for kids to eat well. After they had eaten the apples, she gave them all free chips. She knew it was important to be liked!

Lisa pulled Paula to one side.

'Would you say I'm nice to Mark?' she asked.

For once, Paula didn't pretend not to understand her mum. 'Does *he* say you are nice to him?' she asked.

'I've never asked him,' said Lisa.

'Duh.'

Paula stared at Lisa in the way Lisa stared at Paula when they got her school report. She looked a bit sad and cross. The phrase 'could try harder' came to mind.

'You're not awful to him, I suppose.' Paula looked at her feet. This talk was costing her. 'But you don't seem *into* him. Like, when's his birthday?'

'Erm, late March.' Lisa guessed.

'April the first,' said Paula. 'What's his favourite colour?'

'No idea,' said Lisa.

'Or his favourite band?' asked Paula.

Lisa got the point, so she told Paula to go back to school.

Lisa's mum called. She seemed to have forgotten Lisa was forty-two, and felt the need to check up on her as the boss was away.

'Café still standing, is it? You haven't burnt it down?' she asked.

'No,' said Lisa.

'Chip pan fires are very easy to start,' warned Lisa's mum.

'We use oven chips,' Lisa lied.

The phone call was long and one-sided. Lisa served customers, but she let some sausages burn so she told her mum she needed to go.

'It's good to know that you've got Mark,' said Lisa's mum.

'What is this? Love-Mark-Week?' asked Lisa.

'He'll help you cash up tonight. He's good with numbers,' added her mum.

'And I'm not?' said Lisa. She sounded a bit cross.

'Well, no, love, you're not. You're good with customers. Everyone likes chatting to you. But we both know that you re-sat your maths O level twice.' And Lisa still hadn't passed, but her mum didn't add that. She was not a cruel woman.

It took Lisa an hour and a half to cash up at

the end of the day. It normally took Dave thirty minutes. But it added up in the end, so Lisa was happy. And they had taken a lot of money. It was a good day.

As Lisa left the café and set the alarm, Mark turned up.

'All cashed up?' he asked.

'Yup,' said Lisa.

'Well done, love. I knew you'd do really well.' That was nice, because no one else seemed sure. 'Here.'

Mark pushed a bunch of flowers under Lisa's nose. They were a mixture of roses and that tiny white-flowered stuff called babies' breath.

'They're so lovely,' said Lisa. She gave him a great big kiss. She usually didn't like to kiss in public. But today she thought it was OK.

The roses were pink.

'Pink is my favourite colour,' said Lisa.

'I know,' said Mark.

'What's your favourite colour, Mark?'

'Blue.'

'And what's your favourite band?' asked Lisa.

'Red Hot Chilli Peppers,' he said.

On the way home Mark listed his five favourite movies. Lisa and Mark had three in common. Not bad!

8

24 October

When Lisa had said she'd look after the café
for the week, she'd forgotten it was half-term.
She'd had to farm out the kids to anyone who'd
have them or drag the youngest two into the
café with her. Jack was pleased. He'd live off
chips if he could. But Paula had suddenly
become a vegetarian. She had found out that
pretty much everything sold in the café had
animal fat in it. Then she started to tell the
customers all about killing animals for food. It
wasn't pretty to listen to. Lisa lost three sales in
five minutes. So she gave Paula a fiver and sent
her to the paper shop. Dave needed a business
to come back to.

Dave and his wife were on a boat, sailing
to Norway. They wanted to see ice and things.
Lisa didn't see the point. You might as well
save your cash and wait for winter. They were
usually snowed in until about May round here.
Besides, Lisa was not a water-baby. Feeding

ducks in the park often made her feel seasick. But then, pretty much everything made her sick at the moment. The vitamins hadn't helped much.

Lisa was just wondering whether to fry more chips for the lunchtime rush when Carol called. Carol only ever called if someone had died, or Lisa had done something Carol didn't like. It meant they talked often. Lisa answered with some fear.

'Gill has told John, and John told me. How could you?' Carol said.

Lisa wondered what was wrong. Since she'd last seen Carol Lisa had visited Gill's hairdresser. She'd had blonde highlights put in. And she'd bought a new winter coat. Why would these things make Carol angry?

'Gill told me about the hairdresser. Mum's hand isn't as steady as it was. She can't keep cutting my hair. You are always saying I should take care of myself,' said Lisa.

'I'm not talking about your haircut. That's good. I mean getting *pregnant*,' said Carol.

'Pregnant?' Lisa said. She was shocked. Jack stared at her. He looked shocked too!

'Who's pregnant?' he asked.

'No one.' Lisa took the phone into the back. 'Gill should write books. She has a wild imagination. It's the menopause. It's early. You said so yourself!' Lisa said.

'Oh. Yes, I did, didn't I?' Carol was pleased. Her confidence in her own diagnosis had returned. 'Thank God for that.' She hung up.

Thanks for your concern!

On Wednesdays the café closed after lunch. Paula told Jack that this was a pre-World War tradition.

'You know, like when Mum was a girl,' she said.

Lisa was too tired to be hurt by this statement. She just wanted to go home. She wanted to drink tea and eat biscuits, and perhaps wrap a blanket around her legs like a really old person. But she felt the kids needed her time.

Then in a flash, like a genie, Mark turned up again. He seemed to have a habit of doing that. He offered to look after the kids for the afternoon.

'You need a break,' he said. That was kind.

'What about your work?' Lisa asked.

'Terry can manage on his own,' said Mark.

Lisa didn't think so. Terry looked about the same age as Kerry. He was in fact twenty. But then, to Lisa, policemen and footballers didn't look old enough to tie their own boots.

They decided to visit the cinema, all of them

together. Paula agreed as long as everyone walked behind her and didn't talk to her. Jack, on the other hand, was really chuffed. He was very happy when Mark bought a family ticket. Lisa liked buying a family ticket too – mostly because it saved three quid and they supersized the popcorn.

The moment the lights went down Lisa fell asleep. She missed all the film. She only woke up when Mark gently nudged her. Jack said she'd been snoring. Nightmare! The nightmare was made worse when Mark said, 'Maybe you should get a test done. Gill might be right.'

Gill must have talked to Mark too! Lisa stared at him. She was too stunned to reply. Her mind was full of slow and painful ways to kill her ex-friend. Lisa didn't feel in control. Not one bit.

9

31 October

It was Hallowe'en, and Lisa was fighting demons of her own.

Keith had called to ask when the kids' half-term was. It made her feel fed up.

'Last week,' Lisa said crossly. She'd left him a lot of messages asking if he'd help out with looking after the kids. The kids liked to go to his place, because you couldn't spit without hitting a flat-screen TV. Keith had not called Lisa back.

'Oh. What a shame. I'd have loved to have them stay,' said Keith.

Clank, clank, what's that I hear? The binmen collecting the rubbish he spouts. She didn't believe him. It was a sort of progress. Now she knew every word he said would be a lie.

'Where were you last week?' Lisa asked.

'The Canary Islands. It's the only place to get any sun this time of year,' said Keith.

The kids would have *loved* that. Suddenly, her

week filled with mornings in the café and afternoon trips to her mum's, the cinema and the swimming-pool seemed dull. Lisa wondered if she could prevent the kids from hearing about Keith's holiday. No, Keith and the Big Breasted Woman probably looked bright orange. And they would make everyone sit through a slide-show of photos of the two of them drinking Bacardi. The poor kids! They'd be hurt.

'How's the DIY course going?' asked Keith.

Mostly Lisa was enjoying it. Although she wasn't talking to Gill any more, since Gill had wrongly told everyone she was pregnant. But she liked the idea that she could cope if she had a DIY problem. Still, she wished it hadn't been Keith's idea to do a course in the first place. He'd been very smug ever since.

'It's OK,' Lisa said. She didn't want to give too much away. But she sounded a bit like Paula.

'I was wondering if you knew much about overflow. We've got a back-up in the down-stairs loo. Do you think you could fix it?' asked Keith. 'It really stinks but I don't want to pay a plumber.'

Lisa thought her sawing skills might finally come in useful. She could cut Keith up into little bits and feed him to wild cats – not that you got many wild cats around there. Luckily the beep-beep of 'call waiting' cut the chat short. Keith was saved by the bell.

The person on the end of 'call waiting' was Lisa's mum. Lisa moaned that Keith could offer the kids more than she could. It left her feeling bad. Lisa's mum pointed out that even though Keith could offer the kids more, he never did.

Lisa then confessed to feeling jealous of the Big Breasted Woman's curtains. In fact she was also jealous of her trim size-ten body, her clothes, the hours she spent at the beautician's and her foreign holidays. But Lisa knew she'd have the best chance of her mum understanding if she stuck to curtains.

'Stop looking over your shoulder at what Keith has. Or what you might have had. Or what you once had. Think about the here and now. You'd be better for it. We all would,' said Lisa's mum. She sounded really cross.

Lisa's mum never got snappy with Lisa. So Lisa felt about an inch tall. She got off the phone as quickly as possible.

Lisa sat still for quite a few minutes and thought about her mum's words. She might have a point. In an effort not to think about Keith's holiday to the Canary Islands, Lisa popped out to the local vegetable shop. She bought a pumpkin to carve with the kids. It would be fun.

Two Elastoplasts and some very bad language later, Lisa had carved a lopsided cat's face. It looked funny, not scary. She told her kids it was the effect she wanted.

'To avoid scaring little kids,' she said.

'Really?' asked Kerry. 'Very thoughtful.'

All three kids agreed to go trick or treating. After all, free sweets are free sweets. Even when you're fifteen. They were less happy with the costumes Lisa had made that afternoon. Woolworths had been emptied by the mums who buy Hallowe'en costumes in August. Lisa's kids had to make do with old sheets and black tights.

While Lisa was out trick-or-treating with the kids, Mark called her on her mobile.

'Have you done the pregnancy test yet?' he asked.

'There's no need,' said Lisa.

'Why, have you er . . . ' said Mark.

'No, not yet. But I'm late because I'm menopausal. I wish everyone would stop going on about it. Why can't I sink into my old age without all this fuss?' Lisa asked crossly. Luckily the kids were fighting over mini Mars bars. They were not paying Lisa much attention.

'Lisa, you're too young to be menopausal. Besides, you look great at the moment. Really glowing. You're being sick and you're late. Those are signs of pregnancy, not the menopause. Why won't you admit it? Would it be so awful?' asked Mark.

At that moment Jack rushed across the road to catch up with his friends. He didn't look for cars.

'Jack, for goodness sake. How many times do I have to tell you? Be careful on roads.'

'Is that your answer?' asked Mark.

'No.' Lisa said.

'Well, what then?' he asked.

'This is nothing to do with you,' said Lisa.

'Lisa, if you are pregnant, this has everything to do with me. Or at least I hope it does. Why are you always pushing me away?'

Was she? Lisa couldn't answer his question. After what felt like about five years of silence, he said, 'Well? Is the idea of being pregnant with my child so terrible? Is that why you are in denial?' He sounded cross, but that couldn't be right. Mark was never cross.

Of course the idea of being pregnant with Mark's child wasn't terrible. The idea was wonderful. But it was a fantasy. It couldn't be true. Lisa thought it was a daft question. She didn't dare tell Mark she'd love to be having his baby. She didn't dare tell him that the idea of starting again was too much to hope for. She no longer dared to want anything that much. So she said nothing. They were both silent for ages.

Then Mark coughed and said, 'I see. Well, call me if you need anything.'

Then he hung up.

Suddenly the ghosts and goblins looked really scary to Lisa.

10

4 November

Kerry came home from school earlier than usual. Lisa was pleased to see her daughter. She could do with a distraction. She had so much that she didn't want to think about right now. Mostly she didn't want to think about Mark.

Hadn't she been proved right after all? He had let her down. He'd vanished: one row and then goodbye. She'd heard nothing from him today. She'd expected him to call the following morning, or at least by lunchtime. It had been four days. Why hadn't he called? It was a good thing she'd never fallen for him. Or at least that he didn't know she had. She would have a cup of tea with Kerry and forget all about Mark. Men – who needed them? She and Kerry would have a chat and a giggle.

But Kerry looked sad and tired. It was clear that she was not in the mood for a giggle.

'What's wrong?' asked Lisa.

'Nothing,' said Kerry.

'You keep saying that. But I don't believe you.'

Kerry gave her mum a 'dirty look' and then said, 'I have homework to do.' She went upstairs without another word.

Clearly something was *very* wrong. Kerry never did her homework when she first came home from school. Normally she had really urgent things to do, like watch TV and talk on the phone to her friends. Sometimes she'd be very, very busy indeed, experimenting with new make-up.

Lisa was about to follow her daughter upstairs when she heard the phone ring. It only rang once before Kerry picked it up upstairs. Kerry would now chat to her friends as normal. Lisa knew better than to try to have a talk with her daughter when Kerry's friends were available. Lisa knew her place!

Lisa killed some time reading the big DIY book that she'd bought. She was now very behind with her homework for the course, which was not a very good position to be in as a mum. She could hardly yell at the kids when she was setting such a poor example.

She needed Mark to explain how to plumb in a washing-machine. Where did the hot pipe go? She wondered if she could ring him. He had said, 'Call me if you need anything.' No. No. She did not need him to explain her home-work.

Lisa could not keep her mind on the book. Gill's words about Mark kept coming back to her. What did she mean, Lisa should enjoy new love? Was what she felt for Mark love? And what had he felt for her?

She'd only been seeing him . . . well, a year. A year. That surprised Lisa. She hadn't realized it had been so long.

But they were casual. They only met up about once a week. Lisa thought about it. That wasn't true. Mark stayed at her house most nights now. When he wasn't there she looked for him.

But they'd never talked about love – except when Lisa said she didn't believe in romantic love, which she often said.

Lisa knew what she must do. She had to confront this. She must get straight on the phone and call . . . Gill. To ask her exactly what she meant.

Lisa picked up the phone and realized straight away that Kerry was still on the line. She was about to hang up when she heard Kerry say, 'A baby will ruin my life.'

A baby!

Lisa knew it was a bad thing to listen in to other people's phone calls. But this was her fifteen-year-old daughter talking about *a baby ruining her life*. All rules were made to be broken!

Lisa hardly breathed. If Kerry knew she was listening she'd go mad, and most importantly she'd stop talking.

The other voice on the telephone was Amanda, Kerry's best friend.

'Are you sure?' Amanda asked.

'All the symptoms are there. Tiredness, mood swings and the usual one.'

'Late?'

'Yes. The worst of it is Mum hasn't even noticed! Or if she has she's not saying anything.'

Lisa gasped. Her little girl was pregnant! How could this be? Well, she knew how it happened, but how had it happened to Kerry? They'd talked about this sort of thing last year. Lisa had said if Kerry ever wanted to have sex she should come to her first. They would go to the doctor's together. She'd thought she'd been an open and friendly mum.

But then she had also said that she really, really didn't think Kerry should have sex until she was twenty-five! Maybe that had been a bit unrealistic. Maybe she had sounded too scary. And now look! Kerry had slept with someone and got pregnant.

The stupid girl! The poor girl!

Lisa wanted to run straight upstairs and fling her arms around her little girl. Or fling something heavy at her. She wasn't sure which. She wanted to hold Kerry tightly in her arms and tell her it would be all right. She wanted to kill her.

Lisa took a deep breath and did nothing.

Amanda said, 'What about the dad?'

'He's OK. I actually quite like him,' said Kerry.

Lisa wanted to scream. Kerry quite liked the dad! *Quite liked*. What the hell was she doing sleeping with someone she quite liked? Shouldn't they have been madly in love? That would have been better. But would it? They were children. How could this be made better at all?

'I just never thought he'd be around forever,' said Kerry. She didn't sound sad. Surprised was more like it.

Stupid, stupid girl. Of course he'd be around forever now! Lisa put down the phone and thought about what she should do next.

11

Lisa's first thought was that she wanted to ring Mark. He'd know what to do, what to say. He didn't have kids of his own but he always made things better with her kids. He'd been doing just that for a year now.

But she couldn't call Mark. Yes, he'd said she should call if she needed anything. And yes, this was way more important than help with homework. But Lisa could not call. She had pushed Mark away. She had taken him for granted, just like Gill said. Even Carol had noticed Mark's strengths before Lisa had. Now Lisa had noticed them, and it was too late.

She could not land this trouble at his door. Kerry wasn't even his daughter.

Should Lisa call Keith? Kerry was Keith's daughter. But Lisa knew that the idea of calling Keith was a joke. He didn't return her calls when she wanted to talk to him about childcare

67

over the half-term holiday. He was unlikely to return her calls over something so big. He wasn't good with responsibility.

It was up to her, and her alone. That was OK. She was a good parent, but perhaps not good enough, considering her teenage daughter was pregnant. Lisa couldn't help but blame herself. But Lisa was all Kerry had right now. So she'd have to do.

Lisa slowly climbed the stairs. It was the most terrible walk of her life. How had this happened? Had she let Kerry down? Had she failed to spot the signs that this was going to happen? But what were the signs she was supposed to look for?

A big, flashing one would have been handy.

Kerry was a bright, hard-working, kind girl. Yes, she had the odd teenage tantrum. There were moments when she was selfish with her brother or sister. There were times when she lost her temper, and she had lost her phone more times than Lisa could remember.

But Kerry wasn't daft.

Although, clearly, she was.

Lisa had been thinking about herself too much, and not enough about Kerry. Lisa had been worrying what would happen when the kids left home. She should have been worrying about what was going on under her roof right now!

For example, where had Kerry been when Lisa was at the DIY classes? What was the name of Kerry's boyfriend anyway? Was he her boyfriend? Wasn't he supposed to be 'hanging out' with Chloe Jackson now?

Regret tore at Lisa's heart. She loved being a mum. But it was hard work, harder work than anything else. She didn't want her little girl to have to work that hard yet. She wanted Kerry to do A levels, to get a good job, to wear nice suits and fancy shoes.

But then grandchildren were a blessing. Weren't they? Yes? No? Not like this?

Lisa didn't know the answer, but she was standing outside Kerry's bedroom door. She knew she had to go in there and seem as though she had some ideas at least. Ideas, if not answers.

Lisa knocked and then walked straight in.

Kerry was lying on her bed doing her homework. Lisa was about to say, 'You should sit at your desk to do that. Your handwriting will be neater.' That was what she always said when she found the kids doing their homework on their beds, or in front of the TV, or on their laps. She stopped herself. It didn't matter how neat Kerry's writing was, considering the situation. Kerry's skinny body looked childlike and Lisa could not believe it was capable of carrying a baby.

Lisa looked around her daughter's bedroom. It was the usual mess. There were clothes all over the floor. The walls were full of posters of boy-bands. There were books and dolls on the shelves next to bags of cheap make-up. Kerry hadn't played with dolls for years. But she hadn't got round to throwing them out either. The sight of the dolls made Lisa want to cry.

'I know,' said Lisa. She thought it was best to get straight to the point.

'Know what?' asked Kerry. 'The answers to my homework? I doubt it. I'm doing equations.'

'About the baby,' said Lisa.

'Finally!' said Kerry. She didn't sound scared, or ashamed or worried. She sounded relieved.

Lisa thought that was good. She didn't want an old-fashioned relationship with her daughter. It was good that her daughter was relieved that the truth was now out in the open. Kerry clearly thought her mum would help her. Lisa planned to do just that. Now they could talk honestly about the situation – as equals, as friends.

70

But shouldn't she be a tiny bit worried? Kerry was *fifteen*. All thoughts of equals and friends went from Lisa's head.

'How could you be so stupid?' Lisa yelled. 'You've ruined your life. It's all over. Forget any thoughts about A levels and university. This isn't a game, you know!'

Kerry looked confused.

'Did you think everything would carry on as before? Did you think I'd look after the baby?'

'Well, yes,' said Kerry. 'What else?'

For a second Lisa couldn't speak. She was so angry. Of course she would help with her grandchild, but Kerry was just assuming! Why wasn't she more sorry?

'And what's the father's name?' asked Lisa.

'Well, if you don't know, how should I?' said Kerry.

'Don't you dare be so cheeky.' OK, so Lisa had forgotten Kerry's boyfriend's name. Maybe she hadn't taken enough interest. But Kerry had no right to be so rude!

'Mum, will you stop shouting,' said Kerry. She stood up and closed the bedroom window. 'This is embarrassing enough. We don't want the neighbours hearing before they have to.'

'I think I'm due a bit of a rant!' said Lisa.

71

'Look, I know it must be a bit of a shock,' said Kerry carefully.

'A *bit* of a shock?'

'It's not the end of the world – not the ideal age, but worse things happen,' said Kerry. She sounded relaxed. She sounded grown-up. Lisa felt like the teenager. She was so confused!

Lisa gulped for air. How come her daughter was so calm about this? Didn't she understand how huge this was? Or at least how huge she was going to become. Lisa thought the idea of getting so big would at least cause a reaction. Usually Kerry worried if she ate a Smartie.

'So have you done the test?' asked Kerry.

'Have I done the test?' said Lisa. Her confusion doubled.

'How far gone are you?' asked Kerry.

'How far gone am *I*?' said Lisa. Totally puzzled.

'Mum, why do you keep repeating what I've said? You are acting really strangely. Is it your hormones? Is this another side-effect of your pregnancy?' asked Kerry.

'*My* pregnancy? What are you talking about? *I'm* not pregnant. *You* are,' said Lisa.

Kerry looked as though her mum had hit her. Her mouth hung open with shock.

'I am not!'

'You don't need to pretend, there's no point. I heard you on the phone, talking to Amanda,' said Lisa.

'What exactly did you hear?' Kerry was pink with fury and embarrassment.

'You said, "A baby will ruin my life."'

'Your baby!' said Kerry. 'I was talking to Amanda about *your* baby. A *private* conversation as it happens!' Kerry sounded *very* put out.

'But you were talking about the symptoms. Tiredness and mood swings,' said Lisa.

'*Your symptoms*!' yelled Kerry. 'Mum, how can you be this blind? How can you think I might be pregnant? I don't even have a boyfriend. I've never even . . .' Kerry stopped. She couldn't bring herself to say it to her mum. Not even after their weird conversation. 'You are pregnant. Everyone thinks so but you!'

12

5 November

Normally, Lisa loved bonfire night. Even when it was cold and wet, which was always. She loved the smell of hot-dogs and onions. She loved the noise. She loved the colour. It was exciting. But now, and forever more, she would associate fireworks night with a blind terror.

She'd done the test, finally. Three times in fact. She'd seen women on TV doing the pregnancy test lots of times. In those Sunday night dramas or the soaps. She'd thought it was silly. Those tests cost a fortune. No one in their right mind really wasted money checking the results. It said on the packet 99.999999% correct – or something. But now she got it. That was just it. *People in their right minds* wouldn't do a £10 test three times. But she wasn't.

In her right mind, that was.

She was pregnant.

Age forty-two, plus three almost grown-up

kids, plus not married, plus pregnant, equals big mess.

Despite her lack of maths O level, Lisa thought she was probably ten weeks pregnant. When she'd been pregnant with Kerry, Paula and Jack she'd picked up the phone and told everyone straight away. This time she wanted to hide in a dark room. She'd like to give birth secretly. She could pretend she'd found the baby on the doorstep.

What would Paula and Jack say? What would her family say? Each question made her feel sicker, which was odd when you think she'd felt sick for weeks. Kerry wasn't speaking to her. She was too hurt and embarrassed by Lisa's mistake to talk again, probably. Still, at least that was one less person shouting at her. Lisa thought they might all shout.

Lisa and the kids walked home from the firework display in a moody silence. The odd lone firework flashed in the sky. When Lisa was younger she'd thought fireworks were like little bits of magic exploding into the air. Now, she jumped with every bang.

It took all her nerve to call Gill. Gill was great, and didn't mention the fact that they hadn't really been speaking since Gill had suggested Lisa might be pregnant.

'Congratulations. I knew it!' said Gill. She sounded so happy.

'I didn't,' said Lisa. She sounded so unhappy.

'Really?' asked Gill.

'Really.'

'You were in denial?'

'Yes,' Lisa said.

'But you are pleased.' Gill said it like it was not a question.

Of course everyone assumed Lisa would be pleased. Lisa was a great mum. She always had been. And Lisa liked being a mum. She always had done. What's not to like? And a baby with a good-looking man like Mark – it had to be good news.

Lisa wasn't so sure. Things weren't quite so clear-cut.

'Well . . . yes and no. On a simple level, it's a new life – hurrah! More realistically, I'm an over-the-hill divorcee. I thought the next pram I'd be pushing would be my grandchild's. I'm pretty sure my kids had the same view. Kerry has been upset for weeks because she feared this. Her friend Amanda had just talked her round to the idea when I . . .' Lisa didn't finish the sentence. Her mistake was too silly. 'I don't think the other two will be happy either. Then there's my parents and sister. They are very old-fashioned on such subjects. I'm not married!'

'Who cares about that nowadays?' asked Gill.

'Like I said, they do,' said Lisa.

'And Mark?' asked Gill.

'Mark has vanished,' said Lisa very sadly. This was the worst. How could she have let that happen?

No word from him for nearly a week. There was suddenly a big gap where he used to be. Jack struggled with changing the tyre on his bike. Paula was miserable tonight, because they'd gone to the local fireworks without him. She kept pointing out dads carrying kids on their shoulders. Even though, in heels, she was almost as tall as Mark. He was never going to carry her on his shoulders. He would have bought her a toffee apple though, Lisa had to admit that. Kerry had locked herself in her room for days. Lisa didn't know what to say to get her out. Mark might have known.

Then there was Lisa.

Lisa missed him. How unfair! After all her care to stop herself getting involved, he had still got under her skin. Last night she'd set a place for him at tea out of habit. She missed his chatter. She missed him checking that the doors were locked at night. She could do it

77

herself. She always had. But she liked him doing a double check. She missed his daft jokes. She missed him yelling at the TV. It was beginning to dawn on her that more than anything individual, she missed the chance that he was – another chance at a happy ever after.

'And now there's a baby who will miss his dad more than anyone,' said Lisa, fighting tears.

'Call him,' said Gill.

Lisa didn't think she could. Having had nearly a week to think about it, she now saw that she hadn't been a great girlfriend. Mark was a decent bloke. He'd done nothing to hurt Lisa. He'd done quite a lot to make her life better. But her careful ways must have seemed cold and rude. She hadn't trusted him. She had punished him for all Keith's wrongdoings.

She'd never told him she loved him. She'd said she didn't even believe in that sort of love. But she did love him. How silly it had been to keep that to herself. It was not possible to call him now, just because she was pregnant. She wasn't a helpless, fallen woman. She didn't need saving!

Well, maybe she did, but just a little bit. She did feel very alone, despite the new life inside her – or maybe because of it.

13

6 November

The kids were at their dad's, so Lisa went to bed early. She had to think what she should do next. She rubbed her stomach so that the poor little thing felt OK. She didn't want the baby to have any idea of the trouble that would be coming with it. Lisa was a single mum of three kids – what did one more matter? But it did matter. Lisa didn't want to do this on her own. She wanted her baby to have the best in life and, she thought, maybe Mark was that.

Why hadn't she thought that last week? The timing would have been so much more handy!

Riiiiiiiiiiiiiiinng! The doorbell woke her up. Confused, Lisa pushed through the fog of sleep. She went downstairs to answer it. It was probably Kerry. Maybe she'd forgotten an eyeliner or something.

It was Mark.

Mark stood on the doorstep. Suddenly he seemed taller and broader than ever. Lisa stared at him. Somewhere deep in her mind and her heart she admitted something to herself. Mark looked safe. He looked like someone she could trust. He also looked quite sexy. Well, OK, very sexy. It was probably her hormones. But maybe not. He looked safe and sexy. How had Lisa let him slip through her fingers?

Had she? Why was he here now? Surely he'd come to make up. Or maybe he'd just come to collect his toothbrush. No, that was unlikely. He could buy another toothbrush. Lisa didn't know what to think.

'Gill called me,' he said.

'Of course she did. Rent a gob,' Lisa said. But really she was happy that her friend had made the call she had wanted to make, but hadn't dared to.

'Were you going to call me?' Mark asked.

'Eventually.' Lisa could not look at him. She looked at her feet.

'When? On our child's eighteenth birthday?' He sounded cross. Lisa felt nervous. This sounded like he *was* just here for his toothbrush, not to get back together.

'I'd have told you before then. Come in, we can't talk about this on the doorstep,' said Lisa.

Mark followed her into the house, but he stood in the hall. He looked out of place and that was a shame. Normally he looked so relaxed in her home that you'd have thought it was *their* home.

'I'll put the kettle on,' said Lisa.

He followed her through to the kitchen. It was a total mess, worse than usual. Lisa had lost all interest in tidying the house since she'd lost Mark. She hadn't made the connection until he was standing there. Now she wished that just once in the last week she'd flung a bit of Fairy Liquid at the odd teacup. She was ashamed of the mess. As if she didn't have enough to be ashamed of already! She put the kettle on and started to clear the pots.

'Leave that,' said Mark.

'I'm just making space for us to sit down.'

Lisa moved plates, cups, newspapers, magazines, a loaf of bread and the ketchup. That was just from one chair! Mark still didn't sit down. It was as though he was making a point. He didn't live here any more. He never had, officially. But they'd all thought of him as one of the family. Lisa hadn't realized it until she'd lost him, or pushed him away. It depended how you wanted to look at it.

'How are you feeling?' Mark asked.

'Pretty sick. But that will probably only last a couple more weeks.' Lisa answered the question knowing Mark was talking about the baby. She also knew that the sickness would last a lifetime if he didn't come back to her. But Lisa didn't add that. It sounded a bit keen.

Mark asked the questions everyone asked. Had she done the test? How many weeks pregnant was she? Was she eating well? He asked all the questions with a serious face. But then he asked a new one.

'Do you wish this baby was Keith's?'

'What?!' Lisa nearly dropped her teacup. 'God, no . . . yuk, yuk!' She could not imagine the idea of her and Keith doing the necessary to make a baby, not any more. She'd done it for years – obviously. But now the idea was alien to her. Lisa pulled a face, as though she was trying to spit out a funny taste.

Mark looked amused.

'OK, OK, I believe you. So why do you hate the fact you are having a baby with me?' he asked.

'I don't! Why do you think that?' asked Lisa. She was surprised.

'Well, for weeks you couldn't even face the idea. When you did finally do the test you kept the result a secret from me. Lisa, you are always pushing me away. You won't even call me your boyfriend. After a year! You forget to invite me to family parties until the last minute. You even picked a night class to make the point that you didn't need my help around the house.'

Suddenly Lisa saw things differently. She saw them how Mark saw them. Oh God, she felt terrible. She'd been terrible.

'No, no, it wasn't like that!' said Lisa. 'I didn't know what to call you. I was worried boyfriend was a bit . . . young.' She wanted to add that she'd have happily called him husband. But again it seemed a bit pushy! 'And I picked a DIY course because I thought you wanted to leave me! I was trying to make that easy for you.'

'You wanted to make it easy for me to leave?' Mark looked confused.

'Well, yes, if you wanted to go,' said Lisa. It sounded silly now. But at the time it had seemed logical!

'But why would I want to go?' asked Mark.

'I don't know.' Lisa stopped. She took a deep breath and then said, 'Keith did.' There! Lisa had spat out her fear at last.

Mark could have reacted in one of two ways. He might have shouted that he was not Keith. That he was sick of being punished for Keith's crimes. Or he might just pull her into his arms and tell her not to be a daft cow – which is what he did. But he said 'daft cow' in a nice way so she knew everything was all right. After all, he was male and not able to make long romantic speeches. But Mark was grinning from one ear to the other.

Since he took that so well, Lisa carried on. 'I didn't want you to feel trapped. Everyone has been going on about how old I am. You're younger. I didn't want to make you feel you were stuck with us all. We come as a package deal. Me and the three kids.'

'Four kids now,' said Mark. But he didn't look worried.

They moved through to the front room. They cuddled up on the sofa. Mark put on the TV. He'd clearly done enough talking for one night – probably enough for a lifetime.

'I'm sorry I didn't call you straight away,' said Lisa. 'I should have.'

'Yeah, you should have,' said Mark, and he smiled. 'You know I'm good at fixing stuff.'

The feelings of fear and loneliness began to fade. It seemed that Lisa had got it wrong again. She'd thought Keith was for life but she was wrong about that. Then she'd thought Mark was a stopgap or the rebound. But maybe she was wrong about that too.

'What do we do next?' asked Lisa.

'There's plenty of time to think about

names,' said Mark. 'Put your feet up. I'll make you beans on toast with Cheddar melted on the top, your favourite. There's plenty of protein in that. It's good for the baby.'

14

15 November

Mark's happy and supportive response to the news of the baby gave Lisa a bit of hope that being a forty-two-year-old mum was going to be OK after all. At least she now knew that Mark would help, but Lisa was not in the clear yet.

Lisa and Mark decided that they needed to see a midwife before they told anyone else, to be on the safe side. These days, younger, more excitable girls seemed to tell everyone about their babies six minutes after conception. Lisa would have been happy to wait the full forty weeks. She could just say she was eating too many pies.

Mark said Lisa needed to face her future.

'You sound like my sister!' said Lisa.

'Just because your sister says something doesn't mean it's wrong,' said Mark. 'She thinks I'm great and I am.'

Lisa had to smile.

They made an appointment with the midwife and the shame began.

Co-parenting might be very modern and accepted down south, or in big cities. But there, in a tiny village near Leicester, it was a different story. The local midwife was Jane Davis. Lisa had gone to school with Jane, but they had never been friends. Jane had been good at maths but never let Lisa copy her homework. Lisa had been captain of the netball team but had never picked Jane. That was a decision Lisa regretted now, as Jane raised an eyebrow and noted that Lisa and Mark had different names and addresses.

'And will these addresses be the same at the time of the birth?' Jane Davis asked. She was as good as holding a shotgun to Mark's head. 'How's Keith, then, Lisa? I haven't seen him for a while,' added Jane.

'You're a midwife,' Lisa pointed out. 'He's unlikely to need your services.'

It was not the moment for Lisa to defend herself, or to tell Jane about the Big Breasted Woman and the upset she'd caused. After all, Lisa was flat on her back with her legs in stirrups. And she'd just handed over a pot of wee. It was not a position of strength.

'Well, having this baby won't be the same as

the others,' said Jane Davis. She glumly shook her head. 'You're a very, very old mum, now.'

Lisa had thought the same thing but was cross to hear Jane Davis say it.

'I'm not that old,' said Lisa. 'Loads of women my age or older have babies. Madonna was older.'

'You are hardly Madonna,' said Jane.

Lisa thought that, while this was true, it didn't need saying. She listened crossly as Jane listed lots of scary tests that were needed because of her age. She felt dizzy. Mark suggested they go for a drink. Jane pulled a funny face. Mark turned red and said he meant orange juice.

The chat with Lisa's mum didn't go much better.

'I'm pregnant,' said Lisa.

'Funny thing, dear, I thought you said you were pregnant,' her mum laughed. 'I must have my hearing checked.'

'I *am* pregnant,' said Lisa

'When's the wedding?' asked her mum.

'We haven't talked about a wedding.'

'Give me Mark's address and I'll send your father round.'

Lisa's dad was only five foot nine in his prime. He weighed less than Lisa did on her wedding day. Mark was six foot one and beefy. Lisa didn't think sending her dad round to Mark's was a good idea, although it showed a certain sweetness in her parents' relationship.

Lisa told her mum she didn't want to get married. And that the baby, while not planned, was still great news. And that Mark and Lisa would be very happy co-parenting from different homes. After all, Keith and Lisa did it with the other three.

Lisa thought she sounded believable. Her mum tutted. She wanted to be angry at Lisa, but was secretly excited at the idea of knitting bootees. Also she was trying to stop herself laughing because Lisa had used the term 'co-parenting' – Lisa who had problems with the expression 'partner'!

'I wonder what Carol will have to say,' said Lisa's mum.

Lisa's blood ran cold.

Lisa didn't have to break the news to Carol, though, because by the time Lisa dialled Carol's number, she found her mum had already passed on the good news.

'You lied to me!' said Carol.

'No, I was mistaken,' said Lisa.

'How could you be so stupid?' asked Carol.

'It happens!' said Lisa.

'Yes, to teenagers. Not to *old* women.'

Lisa slammed down the phone. If she'd been able to, she'd have rammed it down Carol's throat.

15

15 November

Mark and Lisa brought home a maxi-size KFC
bucket. There was enough to feed an army.
They encouraged the children to drink pop
and have seconds of ice-cream. Jack sensed a
moment of weakness and asked for a puppy
again. Mark held Lisa's hand. He muttered that
he was right by her side. But he looked more
sick than she did in the mornings.

'Are you splitting up?' Jack asked when he
saw the junk food and fizzy pop.

'No, no,' Lisa said, somewhat bothered by his
train of thought.

'Are you pregnant?' Paula asked the question
but then laughed out loud. She clearly did not
see it as a serious possibility. Kerry glared at Lisa
and Mark, waiting for them to admit the truth.

'Er. Yes,' said Lisa.

The laughter stopped.

'I hate you,' both the younger children said
at once.

'To think that in the past you've prayed that they'd agree on something,' said Kerry. Lisa thought Kerry was enjoying this. She still hadn't forgiven Lisa for thinking she was the one having an unplanned baby.

'I thought you liked Mark,' said Lisa. And that was a bit tactless, considering he was in the room.

'We do. It's just that now everyone will know you're still having sex,' said Paula. She was fighting tears.

'People might have thought so anyway. I'm only forty-two.' Lisa tried to stay calm.

'There's no *only* about it. You're really, really old,' said Paula.

Lisa was getting used to people saying this. An odd thing was happening though, because the more people said it, the less she believed it.

'You're old *and* disgusting,' added Jack. 'I'm going to live at Dad's.'

Lisa wanted to tell him that his dad had sex too, but she couldn't be that cruel.

Paula and Jack got up and marched out of the room. Paula slammed the door with great force. A crack ran from the door-frame across the ceiling.

'That didn't go too badly,' said Mark.

'Rather well, considering,' added Kerry.

Lisa asked Mark to pass the chips. She wished she was the sort of woman who ate *less* under stress.

16

28 November

It was just under a month until Christmas, but there was no sign of peace and goodwill in Lisa's house. The shops were stacked with bubble bath and chocolate boxes, so it had to be the season to be jolly, but it was hard for Lisa to agree.

Lisa and Carol were talking on the phone. They were trying to decide who should buy what for their parents. Last year both women had bought their mum a blender and their dad whisky. It hadn't made for a festive Christmas.

'I've bought Mum a skirt from Next and Dad a jumper,' said Carol.

Lisa bet that Gill had given Carol a staff discount, but didn't say so.

'I won't buy them clothes then,' said Lisa. She had no idea what she would buy them. She had too much on her mind to think about gift-buying.

'Christmas is a magical time,' said Carol with a sigh.

'I know. Usually I like everything about it. From choosing, buying and wrapping gifts, to cooking, over-eating and over-drinking. I really love my old Christmas tree that I drag out of the loft every year. Almost as much as I love my kids,' said Lisa.

'Your Christmas dinners are better than anyone's,' said Carol. Lisa thought it must have cost Carol to be so kind.

'But this year I'm looking forward to Christmas about as much as the turkeys are,' said Lisa, sadly.

At least Paula and Jack had not moved out. They had tried it, but after an evening of hearing the Big Breasted Woman repeat, 'Well, who would have believed it?' they got bored and came home. There was no point in having flat-screen TV if you couldn't hear it above her chat.

They still weren't speaking to Lisa though, apart from barking the odd instruction about what they wanted in their lunchboxes, or asking whether such-and-such a top was clean. In many ways it was a normal situation, except that Lisa knew they were hurt and confused. She hadn't meant to, but she'd turned their world upside-down. It had never been her plan.

Lisa tried to talk to Paula about making the best of things. Lisa confessed to being secretly excited about the thought of once again going to Nativity plays. Paula stared at Lisa, clearly furious.

'Kerry told me what you thought of her!' Paula yelled angrily. 'You didn't like the idea of her being pregnant, did you?'

'Not at all,' Lisa said, 'but Kerry is fifteen.'

'And you are forty-two!' said Paula. Lisa really hadn't known how ageist her family was. 'And you're not even getting married!'

Or how traditional it was.

The thing is Mark hadn't asked her. She couldn't admit as much to Paula. She couldn't risk Paula turning her hate on to Mark, so she stayed quiet.

Mark had said that he wanted to be at the birth classes. But they hadn't discussed anything after that. The truth was, Mark hadn't asked to be a daddy, had he? Why should he want anything more than the birth classes? Lisa told herself she shouldn't care. But she did!

She blamed Christmas. It came with daft hopes, like families sitting around the fireplace, or belting out a chorus of 'Jingle Bells' around the piano, even though everyone knew the best they could hope for nowadays was a row over the remote control.

On a much smaller scale, Lisa was worried about what to buy Mark for Christmas: a Red Hot Chili Peppers album? Or maybe, socks, tie and a pipe? That should give the right message. Lisa couldn't think about it any more because she was attacked by another round of sickness.

'Tis the season to be jolly.

Yeah, right.

17

This year Christmas shopping was a chore. Lisa was so tired. She looked like the walking dead, and she felt about as healthy too. When she wasn't being sick, she felt sick. Carol claimed to have the same problem – she said it was the shame.

Carol wasn't going to serve drinks during the break at her kids' Christmas concert this year. She always did. But she said this year she wouldn't be able to hold her head up in public when Lisa's news broke. Lisa sarcastically thanked her for her support and asked if she'd kept any of Katie's baby equipment. Lisa couldn't afford to take offence. Carol said she'd check in the garage but she wasn't hopeful.

'You'd like to cut me off completely, wouldn't you?' said Lisa.

'Yes, but it's your turn to host Christmas,' said Carol. Lisa wasn't sure if she was joking. Carol hated cooking and would eat with the devil if it saved her from washing up greasy pans.

Lisa's mum kept saying that she was looking forward to Christmas dinner, as she'd be 'glad to talk some sense into Mark'. Lisa was worried that her mum and dad would turn up with a few pounds of potatoes and some carrots from Dad's allotment. They'd offer them up as a dowry.

Money was tight now that Lisa had the new baby to plan for. Buying gifts on a budget for her disapproving family was no fun at all. Lisa walked around stores that sold scarves and novelty cufflinks. She didn't know anyone who wore either. Still, that hadn't stopped her buying similar gifts in the past.

Lisa was walking around New Look, deciding whether to buy Kerry and Paula trendy, skimpy tops. That way she'd get into their good books. But maybe she should stick to her motherly instincts and buy them thermal vests? Her brother called to ask Lisa what he should buy Gill for Christmas.

'As in my friend, Foghorn Gill?' asked Lisa.

'One and the same,' said John.

'In that case, buy her a gag.'

'With a blindfold and handcuffs do you think?' asked John.

Lisa didn't quite get his meaning. But she thought it was likely to be sexual. What else would it be with John? She blushed. 'Too much information,' she said.

Suddenly Lisa had some idea how her kids felt about her and Mark. There were some people it was best never to imagine having sex: your parents, your children, any of your relatives, come to think of it! That's what made a happy family.

'By the way, I'm bringing Gill and her boys to the annual chimps' tea party on Christmas Day,' said John.

Lisa couldn't remember John bringing a date to Christmas dinner before. It must be serious with Gill.

Lisa moved on to Debenhams. She was choosing between a fake-fur hot-water-bottle cover and a Christmas cracker full of miniature whisky bottles when she bumped into Mark.

'What are you doing in town?' she asked.

'Shopping.'

Of course, he probably was. They were in a shop. But he looked shifty and Lisa doubted him. Shouldn't he be at work? Lisa looked round to see if she could spot a leggy blonde. Maybe he had a secret meeting, with a secret woman.

'Who are you looking for?' asked Mark.

Lisa was too tired to fake it. 'Your mistress,' she said.

Mark laughed. 'I love your sense of humour.' Then he saw her stony expression. 'You are joking, aren't you?'

'I always expect the worst, and I'm rarely disappointed,' said Lisa. She knew she was falling into her old habit of punishing Mark for Keith's crimes. It was wrong of her. But it was a hard habit to break.

Mark looked cross for a second. But then he just asked what Lisa had bought. He was not impressed by the mittens for her mum, or by the dancing Santa for Carol, even if it did light up. Lisa didn't like it much either, but Carol would hate it. That was what was good about it.

Lisa's mobile rang again. This time it was Keith to say he and the Big Breasted Woman were pleased to accept the kids' invitation to Christmas dinner. The kids had invited him to annoy Lisa. Obviously, it was an act of war. And Keith said he'd bring his parents.

Clearly, they all wanted to be in on the family crisis and gossip. Nothing else would make the Big Breasted Woman give up staying in the five-star country hotel. This had been her

101

plan for Christmas. She'd said that the hotel served mince pies and mulled wine, in front of the fire, at midnight on Christmas Eve. Very traditional and costly but worth every penny, said the Big Breasted Woman. Lisa had a Christmas Eve tradition too. She defrosted the turkey with a hairdrier and cursed that all the shops were closed. She always ran out of sticky tape when she still had a mountain of wrapping to get through.

'Damn!' said Lisa as she hung up the phone. 'I wish mobile phones had never been invented. Then I wouldn't get bad news in Debenhams. Christmas Day will be like Paula's birthday – but worse because now I'm a fallen woman! We'll have to sit together and listen to the Queen's speech on traditional values.'

'It will be OK,' said Mark

'I can't even drink to numb the pain.' Lisa did the maths. She'd be sixteen weeks pregnant by then. She'd be at the looking-fat-but-not-looking-pregnant stage – great.

Lisa started to cry quietly. Mark pulled her to his chest. This made her feel better – and then worse. Hadn't he noticed that it was nice when they were together?

'Do you want to see what I bought?' asked

Mark. He pulled out two vouchers for a day of pampering at a spa. 'One each for Kerry and Paula, for Christmas.'

Lisa was touched by his thoughtfulness, and his planning. Fancy, a man who Christmas shops in early December. Keith never bought Christmas presents. Lisa got new carpets in the January sales every three years. Keith got a good staff discount. Lisa bought the presents for everyone else. Lisa's dad and John bought gifts from the petrol station on Christmas Eve. Lisa's mum had three torches, ten cans of de-icer and loads of packets of those hanging air-freshener things. Lisa's mum was never ungrateful though. She said she was the woman to know if ever you found yourself in a dark, snowy, smelly place.

'This is for Jack,' said Mark. He opened another shopping bag. Lisa looked inside.

'A belt?' she asked.

'A lead. And I thought we'd get him the dog to go with it. I know we have a lot on with the baby and things, but he really wants a dog. I'll walk it. Every family needs a dog,' said Mark.

Jack had been pleading for a dog for months. He'd been going on and on and on and on. But

Lisa had been firm: no, no, no. But that last sentence from Mark changed her mind.

Every *family* needs a dog.

18

11 December

Lisa and Mark returned from the animal rescue centre. They'd picked a bouncing black and brown pup. The lady at the animal rescue said she was a cross between a Labrador and a Bulldog.

'Lord help us,' said Lisa. But she couldn't resist. The dog had nice eyes.

The kids were all at home watching TV. The scene would have been perfect if Lisa and Mark had found the kids doing their homework. But, hey, you have to be realistic.

Jack and the dog jumped joyfully around the kitchen. One shouted thank you a million times. The other dripped saliva on Lisa's lino. Even the girls managed a smile.

'What should we call her?' asked Jack.

'It's your dog, you pick,' said Lisa.

'No, Mark can pick and I'll pick the name for the baby,' Jack said with a big grin.

This was the first thing he'd said that so

much as hinted that he was accepting, or looking forward to, the baby. Jack had guessed Mark's part in getting Lisa to agree to the dog. He'd be grateful forever.

'Nothing obvious like Snowy,' said Paula.

'The dog's not white, therefore Snowy isn't what you'd call obvious,' argued Jack.

'Except, it's snowing,' said Kerry.

They all rushed to the window and silently huddled together. Kerry was right. Suddenly Christmas seemed closer and there was a sense of magic and joy in the air. They all stayed together and looked out of the window for ages. They looked like one big happy family.

'What about Tiger?' suggested Jack.

'I hope he means for the dog, not the baby,' said Paula. She gave Lisa a shy smile. Lisa didn't need to hear the words. She knew Paula was also saying that she was OK with the idea of a baby after all. Lisa felt relief wash over her.

'How about Daisy?' said Kerry.

'Daisy Dog is really girly,' said Jack.

'I meant for the baby!' said Kerry.

The happy family moment seemed as though it was going to vanish.

'Mari,' said Mark. Then he coughed and Lisa didn't hear the rest.

Lisa moved away from the window. She

poured five mugs of tea. She poured the right amount of milk and spooned sugar into each mug. Then she passed them round, before she started to hunt in the cupboards for the chocolate biscuits. She'd hidden them from herself in an effort to curb her non-stop eating.

The room was silent. All eyes were on Lisa.

'I like Welsh names. I prefer Mari to Daisy,' said Lisa. 'How about we call the dog Daisy and, if the baby is a girl, we'll call her Mari? If it's a boy, Jack gets to pick. That's fair, isn't it?'

Still no one spoke – clearly everyone was wowed by her clear and firm solution.

'Marry me,' repeated Mark. This time he didn't cough.

19

Of course she said yes. For a moment, the kids worried that she wasn't going to answer, let alone say yes. Mark had to ask the question twice. But she just made him do that because she liked the sounds of the words, 'Will you marry me?'

'Yes. Yes!'

Mark had been a bit more confident that Lisa would say yes. He'd brought a bottle of champagne with him. As he popped the cork, he realized he was the only person in the room who was both legally old enough and not pregnant and could therefore drink it. Still, no one cared. The thought was a good one.

Mark and Lisa married on New Year's Eve, at 5 p.m. It was a candlelit civil ceremony in a country hotel. Lisa thought New Year's Eve was a wonderful evening to marry. Out with the old, in with the new! Mark thought it was a wonderful evening to marry, as he was not likely to ever forget their anniversary. And Lisa's brother, John, voiced the thoughts of all the guests. It was a wonderful evening to marry, as they'd all be getting drunk anyway that night. They might as well do it in candlelight.

It was a smallish wedding, only thirty guests. Lisa and Mark's close families came, and a few friends who were available at the last minute – more than you'd imagine. Most people don't make plans for New Year's Eve until about the 29th of December. Everyone is sure that, at the last minute, they'll be invited to an amazing party. This year, for Mark and Lisa's friends and family, exactly that happened.

Lisa bought a cream dress and jacket from Monsoon. It was a bit expensive but what the hell! If not tonight, then when? She told herself that, as it was floaty, she'd be able to wear it throughout the pregnancy and afterwards. Gill agreed that this was true, because the outfit was cream and baby sick would blend.

The girls wore green velvet off-the-shoulder dresses. Both of them were wild about how grown-up and beautiful they looked. They would have liked to hide their happiness and excitement (as being that happy and excited wasn't exactly cool) but they couldn't. They weren't good enough actresses.

Jack was also impressed with the suit hired just for him. Although Mark, John and Lisa's dad all grumbled about looking like stuffed penguins, Lisa didn't believe them for a moment. She knew they all loved wearing the posh suits. Every one of them thought he was James Bond.

Lisa carried pink roses. She carried them over her bump, because Carol reminded her to do so about fifty times, although it was a mystery as to who exactly Carol thought they were hiding the bump from. The best man's speech was full of jokes about shotgun weddings. The ceremony was short but did the job. The buffet was great and everyone ate until they felt sick. Lisa was pleased – she liked the idea that they were keeping her company.

Lisa felt as though she was walking on air, held up by good wishes from her friends and, most importantly, by hope for her future.

Lisa watched as her mum and dad danced around the disco floor. They danced a slow and old-fashioned dance. It was familiar to her. She'd watched them dance together hundreds of times. Her kids pushed and shoved each other, half kindly, half looking for trouble, on the same dance floor. She'd seen that often enough too. Suddenly Lisa was aware of Mark by her side.

'Happy?' he asked.

She nodded, flushed with how perfect it all was.

'Want to dance?' he asked.

'Can you?' she asked. She was a bit surprised. They'd never danced together.

'I'll hold you. We'll sway. No one will laugh. It's our wedding day.'

Lisa took Mark's hand and followed him on to the floor. There they swayed together. Three generations. One happy family.

Quick Reads

Books in the Quick Reads series

Lose yourself
in a good
book with *Galaxy®*

Curled up on the sofa,
Sunday morning in pyjamas,
just before bed,
in the bath or
on the way to work?

Wherever, whenever,
you can escape
with a good book!

So go on...
indulge yourself with
a good read and the
smooth taste of
Galaxy® chocolate.

Quick Reads ■

Fall in love with reading

Quick Reads are brilliantly written short new books by bestselling authors and celebrities. Whether you're an avid reader who wants a quick fix or haven't picked up a book since school, sit back, relax and let Quick Reads inspire you.

We would like to thank all our funders:

We would also like to thank all our partners in the Quick Reads project for their help and support:

NIACE • unionlearn • National Book Tokens
The Reading Agency • National Literacy Trust
Welsh Books Council • Welsh Government
The Big Plus Scotland • DELNI • NALA

We want to get the country reading

Quick Reads, World Book Day and World Book Night are initiatives designed to encourage everyone in the UK and Ireland – whatever your age – to read more and discover the joy of books.

Quick Reads launches on **14 February 2012**
Find out how you can get involved at www.**quickreads**.org.uk

World Book Day is on **1 March 2012**
Find out how you can get involved at www.**worldbookday**.com

World Book Night is on **23 April 2012**
Find out how you can get involved at www.**worldbooknight**.org

Quick Reads

Fall in love with reading

Doctor Who
Magic of the Angels

Jacqueline Rayner

BBC Books

*'No one from this time
will ever see that girl again . . .'*

On a sight-seeing tour of London the Doctor wonders why so many young girls are going missing. When he sees Sammy Star's amazing magic act, he thinks he knows the answer. The Doctor and his friends team up with residents of an old people's home to discover the truth. And together they find themselves face to face with a deadly Weeping Angel.

Whatever you do – don't blink!

A thrilling all-new adventure featuring the Doctor, Amy and Rory, as played by Matt Smith, Karen Gillan and Arthur Darvill in the hit series from BBC Television.

Quick Reads 📖

Fall in love with reading

The Little One

Lynda La Plante

Simon & Schuster

Are you scared of the dark?

Barbara needs a story. A struggling journalist, she tricks her way into the home of former soap star Margaret Reynolds. Desperate for a scoop, she finds instead a terrified woman living alone in a creepy manor house.
A piano plays in the night, footsteps run overhead, doors slam. The nights are full of strange noises. Barbara thinks there may be a child living upstairs, unseen. Little by little, actress Margaret's haunting story is revealed, and Barbara is left with a chilling discovery.

This spooky tale from bestselling author Lynda La Plante will make you want to sleep with the light on.

Quick Reads 📖

Fall in love with reading

Full House

Maeve Binchy

Orion

**Sometimes the people you love most
are the hardest to live with.**

Dee loves her three children very much, but now they are all grown up, isn't it time they left home?

But they are very happy at home. It doesn't cost them anything and surely their parents like having a full house? Then there is a crisis, and Dee decides things have to change for the whole family . . . whether they like it or not.

Quick Reads

Fall in love with reading

The Cleverness of Ladies

Alexander McCall Smith

Abacus

There are times when ladies must use
all their wisdom to tackle life's mysteries.

Mma Ramotswe, owner of the No.1 Ladies' Detective
Agency, keeps her wits about her as she looks into
why the country's star goalkeeper isn't saving goals.
Georgina turns her rudeness into a virtue when she
opens a successful hotel. Fabrizia shows her bravery
when her husband betrays her. And gentle La proves
that music really can make a difference.

With his trademark gift for storytelling, international
bestselling author Alexander McCall Smith brings us
five tales of love, heartbreak, hope and the cleverness
of ladies.

Quick Reads 📖

Fall in love with reading

Amy's Diary

Maureen Lee

Orion

A young woman finds her way
in a world at war.

On 3rd September 1939 Amy Browning started to write a diary. It was a momentous day: Amy's 18th birthday and the day her sister gave birth to a baby boy. It was also the day Great Britain went to war with Germany.

To begin with life for Amy and her family in Opal Street, Liverpool, went on much the same. Then the bombs began to fall, and Amy's fears grew. Her brother was fighting in France, her boyfriend had joined the RAF and they all now lived in a very dangerous world …

Quick Reads

Fall in love with reading

Quantum of Tweed:
The Man with the Nissan Micra

Conn Iggulden

Harper

Albert Rossi has many talents. He can spot cheap polyester at a hundred paces. He knows the value of a good pair of brogues. He is in fact the person you would have on speed-dial for any tailoring crisis. These skills are essential to a Gentleman's Outfitter from Eastcote. They are less useful for an international assassin.

When Albert accidentally runs over a pedestrian, he is launched into the murky world of murder-for-hire. Instead of a knock on the door from the police, he receives a mysterious phone call.

His life is about to get a whole lot more interesting ...

Other resources

Enjoy this book? Find out about all the others from
www.quickreads.org.uk

Free courses are available for anyone who wants to develop
their skills. You can attend the courses in your local area.
If you'd like to find out more, phone 0800 66 0800.

 Don't get by get on 0800 66 0800

For more information on developing your skills in Scotland
visit www.**thebigplus**.com

Join the Reading Agency's Six Book Challenge at
www.**sixbookchallenge**.org.uk

Publishers Barrington Stoke and New Island
also provide books for new readers.
www.**barringtonstoke**.co.uk • www.**newisland**.ie

The BBC runs an adult basic skills campaign.
See www.**bbc**.co.uk/**skillswise**